Gertrude Kloppenberg (Private)

Ruth Hooker

drawings by
Gloria Kamen

Abingdon Press
Nashville and New York

for
Charlotte, Jane, and Barbara

Gertrude Hoppenberg
(Private)

KEY

Good Day-- ☆

Medium Day----------------------------------- ◯

Bad Day-- ▢

Today I got a notebook. This book. After school I went to the dime store and bought it. On the front I put GERTRUDE KLOPPENBERG—PRIVATE. I wish I had put VERY PRIVATE but now there isn't room.

Every day after school I am going to write in it. When I am through writing I will put it in the bottom drawer of my dresser where Melinda Lou's house is. That's why I bought a black-and-white speckled book. I will turn it upside down and put it under Melinda Lou's table which I made out of a box with matchsticks for legs. It will look like a rug. If anybody looks in my bottom dresser drawer they will say, "Oh, what a nice rug Melinda Lou has," and not know it is really a book. Only nobody ever looks in my bottom drawer because it is very private. But if they did.

I will not write in my book on Saturday or Sunday because those days aren't private enough. Also I will have a

9

thought for every day like in the little book Mother reads. You should have a thought every day I think. Also I am going to mark the top of the page with the kind of day it is (see key in front of book).

Now I am ready to write in my book. It was a good day because I got my book and none of the Murphy boys were in the backyard to bother me when I got home. Now I have to do my three jobs before Mother gets home. I think I hate dusting most.

Thought for the day: Private things are nice.

Yours truly,

Gertrude (sometimes called
Trudy)

Tuesday, March 26

Today was the awfullest day. I had to stay after school to finish my math. I guess I don't pay attention. I tell myself to listen to the teacher and I do. But when she isn't talking I don't keep thinking about what I am doing, like math. No, I do so think about math.

Today I thought what a nice number 7 is. I like it best because nothing can be done to it. Like nothing goes into it. I like the way it looks with its stand-up-straight way and the cap sticking out in front. I tried to make all different looking 7's with the caps different ways. Then Miss Hurly called for the papers and said, "Very well, Gertrude. You may stay after school and finish your paper." I wish somebody would call me Trudy.

Then when I got home the Murphy boys were in the backyard. I could tell before I got there because of the noise. I knew they would call me bookworm and say ugh and wormy old bookworm and things like that because I had some school books. So I had a plan. I put my books under my coat. When I opened the gate there they were, the three middle ones, Don and Bill and Tom.

I thought I was safe because they were busy jumping around. Off and on the porch and on the fence and off. But they saw me. They called me fat and fatso and fatty and I hated it. I kept looking at the ground. Mother says their bark is worse than their bite but I hate their bark. Also Mother says sticks and stones can break your bones but names will never hurt you. But I hate names. I just look at the ground and squinch up inside and go up the back stairs from porch to porch. I want to run, but if I did I think they might chase me and I'd be so scared that I'd scream. I hate it.

I'm going to ask Mother for a key to the front door and then I won't ever have to go through the backyard again as long as I live.

Now I'm late doing my three jobs and I can hardly say hello to Melinda Lou. I think I'll make the square (see key in front of book) black as black because today is worse than bad.

Thought for the day: Names can too hurt.

Yours truly,

Gertrude (who nobody ever
calls Trudy)

Today was a medium day. Now I have used all the signs (see key in front of book) except I changed the bad day to an awful day yesterday by making it black. Maybe I should have more signs.

Last night I asked Mother for a front door key but she said no, it's too dangerous going up those dark stairs. She doesn't know how dangerous it is coming through the backyard with those Murphy boys there. She says it's not nearly so dangerous. She just doesn't know. Also I asked her if I was fat and she said I was well built. I don't know what that means.

I checked at school. I looked at other people's arms and legs and then at my own. I know I'm not fat. But I'm not skinny. Maybe I am fat. I feel fat sometimes. If I was skinny I guess I'd jump around and shout and run a lot. The way I am I like to stand and look and think.

Like last winter when it snowed and snowed. At

13

recess when I stepped out of the door a snowflake fell on my coat sleeve, and for the first time I saw one snowflake all by itself. It was the most beautiful thing I'd ever seen. I never remember seeing anything so pretty before. I stood there all recess watching each snowflake as it fell on my coat. Other kids were throwing snowballs and jumping in drifts. Miss Hurly said, "Now, Gertrude, don't just stand there, you'll get cold." But the bell rang so I didn't have to do anything. I was cold but I had seen a snowflake.

Maybe I'll try running around a little bit tomorrow.

Today I finished my math on time. But I didn't like it. I started thinking about 12, which might be a better number than 7. But in a different way. Then I remembered yesterday and didn't want to go through that again so I did my math.

I decided I would think about 12 when I got home and could be private. So now is the time. What I like about 12 is that it is such a friendly number and can do so many things. It has many parts like 2 and 3 and 4 and 6 and can do almost anything. It's even friends with 8 and 9 and 5 and 7, sort of. It's like Sandra at school who can do almost anything and always has lots of friends around her. But I still like 7.

Also today there was only one Murphy boy when I got home, the oldest one, Bob. He only grunted when I went past. I looked at the ground so I don't know if he grunted at me or something else.

Thought for the day: Today I have no thought. It was too medium a day.

Yours truly,

Gertrude (sometimes known as Trudy)

14

Today I saw something on my way home from school. I had to go back for my spelling book because I forgot tomorrow was spelling test day. I was walking without any kids around. It was a nice day. Just like a March day should be. The wind was blowing but it was pushing me from behind. The sun was shining, but not all the time.

I turned down an alley. It wasn't so blowy in the alley and it was warmer and quieter and like a different place. It was a nice alley. I walked very slow. Then I heard a creaking noise. I looked and a gate in a fence blew open. Inside the fence some little white flowers were growing.

I didn't know flowers grew when it was so cold. They were so pretty I just stood and stared at them. Then the gate blew closed with a bang and I jumped and went away. It must have been a very private garden because the houses were for only one family except for the big building at the end.

15

I almost got lost coming home. I was just so busy thinking about those flowers. But I finally didn't get lost.

When I got near home I heard the Murphy boys shouting. I didn't want to face them. I thought I'd run through the yard and up the stairs before they could see me. But that could be dangerous. I was saved because Mrs. Murphy came out and told them they had to put on their coats or they'd catch their death of cold. They were so busy arguing with their mother that I got safely upstairs without being seen. So today I think I'll put a star on top of this page.

Thought for the day: Flowers are nice.

Yours truly,

Gertrude

Same day, later

Now it is bedtime but I have to write some more. First I am going to put marks around the star like it was shining because it has been better than a good day.

When Mother came home from work she brought something for me. For no reason. Mother and Miss Rice were shopping at lunch hour and they saw it on sale and Miss Rice said, "Go ahead get it. It looks like Gertrude." It was a dress. An extra nice dress. Plaid with a white collar just like pictures of school girls in magazines. And Miss Rice said it looks like me.

I tried it on and looked at my top half in the mirror over my dresser, and then I stood on the bed and looked at my bottom half in the mirror. It looks nice. Then I hung it up on a hanger and I am going to save it for a special day.

Also Mother said that Miss Rice said I should have

a friend. Maybe I will try and find a friend because Miss Rice is head of housewares and knows.

Just now Mother said, "For heavens sake, Gertrude, turn off the light and go to sleep." So I will. She likes the name Gertrude. I wish I did. Mother says most people don't like their own names, but I think I would if they'd only call me Trudy. But I guess they never will.

Second thought for the day: Miss Rice is nice.

Yours truly,

Gertrude

Friday, March 29

Nothing went my way today. First I was late for school. Nobody was walking to school and nobody was on the playground when I got there. It felt like I was the only one in the world. I was scared. I ran and got to my seat just as the tardy bell rang. So I was saved from being tardy but it was awful.

We had the spelling test first thing and I remembered I'd forgotten to study. My plan was to always get 100 but now it's too late.

I couldn't think how to spell cough. I spelled it coff. I should have guessed it was one of those ough words. Whoever thought up how to spell words didn't do a very good job. In my own private book I'm going to spell the way I want to.

I forgot to look for a friend. I did look for the garden on the way home only I couldn't find it. The thing is

19

I can't remember how I walked home yesterday. There are three ways to start to walk home and then different turns along each way. But I will keep looking. Maybe it's a magic garden that's been magicked away. It's very mysterious. When I think about it, the flowers look prettier all the time. They sort of glow in my mind.

None of the Murphy boys were around so I think I'll just put a plain square on top and not make it black.

Thought for the day: Things shood be speld the way they sownd.

Yours truly,

Gertrude

This was April Fool's Day and I couldn't think of a fooling thing all day. Somebody put a plastic ink blot on Miss Hurly's desk and that was sort of funny because she uses ballpoint pens and doesn't have any ink. I told someone their shoe was untied but they said, so what. Maybe I can fool my mother when she comes home but not much or she'll get too excited.

I looked a little for a friend. Sandra has got too many friends already. Barb and Jean are best friends and they always whisper together and I thought, how nice. But there's no room for me because they're too close together.

I saw a girl at the library Saturday where I got two very good books which I have almost read all of. But you can't talk much in the library. Besides I didn't know what to say.

I looked for the garden but didn't find that either. I worried about the flowers because it snowed hard Sunday.

March went out like a lion. I can't remember how it came in but it must have been like a lamb. Maybe I should put down the weather each day but I already have lots of things to put down. Like the kind of day. Today I think is a medium day. I hope those flowers weren't hurt by the snow.

No Murphy boys were out when I got home.

Thought for the day: It's hard to find things when you're looking for them.

Yours truly,

Gertrude

Tuesday, April 2

I forgot about speling the way I want to in my privat book. But now I will start. As I rite I see ther are not many words that need changing because they mostly do spel like they sownd. Some I have got used to speling the way they are. It is mostly the ough words and leaving off some letters that don't get said like the w in write. It is fun but it takes longer to spel this way.

Today I looked som mor for a frend. Patty who sits on the blakboard side of the room and who I hardly know was standing and reeding a book at reces. I trid to be frendly and asked what she was reeding. She said, "None of your busness." She put the book up close to her and hid it with her arms and I went away. What book culd be so secret? Maybe it was a privat book like this one. But why bring it to scool? Asking questuns is not the way to make frends I think.

I fownd the rite alley after scool. I think it is the

one. But I didn't find the garden becas all the gates wer closed. I will look tomoro. Maybe nobody will be in the alley and I can look beter.

The Murphy boys wern't in the bakyard agin today. I wunder where they are?

I am late today becas I stopt at the dime stor for a bag of candy. I have a plan to get a frend. If I stand with a bag of candy at reces maybe somebody will come up and talk to me. I will giv them a peece and we will be frends. Like when you hav penuts in the park and the piguns come.

Now I wil do my three jobs and reed if I get dun in time.

Thought for the day: It is intresting to look for things evn if you don't find them rite away.

Yours truly,

Gertrude

My plan wurkt. At reces Mary Beth came up to me and my bag of candy and sed, "Hello, what you got?" I sed, "Candy, here hav one." But she took two. After she ate the candy I sed, "Can you play after scool tomoro?" She sed, "I got piano lessens." I sed, "It must be fun to play a piano." She sed, "It's boring." Then she sed, "You can come to piano lessen with me if you want." I sed, "I'll ask my mother," and gave her some mor candy. She took three peeces. But maybe I fownd a frend.

Also I fownd the garden. I thot very hard when I walkt down the alley and rememberd where I stopt the first time. I was rite. The gate wasn't open but there was a not hole and I peeked thru it. I had to stand on my toes. I saw the little wite flowers. They are safe. They must be very strong flowers to stand snow. Also I saw more things. It is a very privat garden. It has grass in the midle and places for flowers arownd the

25

edge and it has a bench. Some more things are growing. Some green things are stiking up a ways, sort of thik and in bunches. It looked like a nice place to be.

The Murphy boys weren't in the backyard. Mother sed last nite that they were sik. I am sorry they are sik but it makes it easier for me.

Today was a good day strait thru.

Thot for the day: It is nice to find things.

Yours truly,

Gertrude

Thursday, April 4

Now I am home. Today was an experience. I wore my new dress and Mother was so happy that I had a frend to go to piano lessens with. Mother sed if I didn't have time to do my jobs when I got home she wuld help me. But I did my jobs alredy, very fast. Now I will rite in my privat book until Mother comes home. If Mother is tird and wants to put her feet up and rest until we make diner I will evn rite some more.

Now I am redy to tel what hapend. After scool I met Mary Beth and we started walking to her piano lessen which is on the other side of the scool. First thing Mary Beth sed, "Have you got any more candy?" I did. I took the bag out of my poket and she held out her hand so I poured the peeces in her hand and sed, to be generus, "We can share them." But there were five peeces. "That's not evn," I sed. Then Mary Beth ate one and sed, "Now they are evn." So we each had two peeces. Sum people figur things out very strangly.

Mary Beth was rite about piano lessens. They are very boring. I sat on a bumpy chair in a dark living room. I don't no how it culd be so dark when the sun was shining out-side. But the sun didn't reach that room. Mary Beth's teacher had fuzzy gray hair and glasses at the end of her nose and slippers on. I culd hear Mary Beth playing in the next room very slowly, plunk, plunk, plunk. The teacher kept making Mary Beth do it agin and agin and told her to wach her fingers.

28

It never sownded like music to me. I culd here the teacher tell Mary Beth to practis more. Then Mary Beth was thru and we went outside.

      When we got outside Mary Beth sed, "I've got to go home now." Mary Beth lived farther away from scool than where we were. I didn't know for sure how to get home from there and thot I'd ask Mary Beth to walk back towrd scool part way with me, but she said no she culdn't or she'd be late. So I went by myself. I had luck finding the scool and then I knew how to come home from there.

Well, I thot on my way home from the scool yard, at least I can peek at my privat garden. But some woman was walking her dog rite there so I had to walk by like I was just walking by and nothing else. I culd almost feel those flowers that I culdn't see while I walked by.

At least the Murphy boys weren't out.

I hoped Mary Beth wuld be a frend. I red about two frends once. They were true blue frends. It wasn't an old time story or a fairy story either. They had their ups and downs but they always stuck together. If there was truble they stuck together. When one girl was accused of taking something the other girl believed her while everyone pointed fingers. Together they fownd the real theif and they were true blue frends to the end. I wonder if that story culd ever be true.

Thot for the day: Some stories that sownd like they're true are really fairy stories.

Yours truly,

Gertrude

Friday, April 5

Today I got 100 in spelling. I studied very hard last night after dinner. But then I got a paper back and it was all marked up with big red circles and red lines going to the margin with SP written all over. I had forgot and spelled my own way like I do in my private book. That is why I have given up spelling my own way even in my private book. It is too risky. Like the time I said out loud in class that it was Wednesday and said the D like I do to myself so I can remember how to spell it, and everyone laughed. I guess you have to do the same things in private that you do outside or you might forget and embarrass yourself.

Mary Beth came up to me at recess and said, "Do you have any more candy?" I said, "No." She said, "Oh," and went away. So that's the end of Mary Beth as a friend.

On the way home from school I peeked at my garden again. I can't see everything at once. I have to twist my head and look at one part at a time. I looked for those white flowers. They are almost gone. Then I heard a scratching sound and twisted around and looked and saw a woman. She looked right at the knot hole. She was kneeling and had a plant in her hand that she was tearing apart. The woman had very blue eyes and I thought they were seeing me. I went away as fast and quiet as I could. But now, when I think about it, I don't think she could see my eye in that little knot hole. Next time I won't run away even if she's there. I wonder what she was tearing up a plant for?

The Murphy boys are still sick.

Thought for the day: You can't understand spelling, just learn it.

Yours truly,

Gertrude

Today is Monday and I am writing in my book again. It is raining outside, not hard but it's very uncomfortable and cold. I stopped and looked at my garden and even in the rain it looked nice. Also I saw something new. A batch of yellow flowers very low and bright colored in a corner. I wonder what they are.

When I got home and went to get my book out of my bottom drawer I found Melinda Lou sitting at the table where I left her last Saturday. I forgot to put her to bed. I don't know how I could forget Melinda Lou like that. She means very much to me and I try to take care of her because right now she is the best friend I have.

The Murphy boys are still sick. I saw them at the window but I didn't really look. Saturday I made some cookies and Mother said to take some downstairs to the Murphys. I didn't want to but Mother was busy scrubbing the bathroom so

I did. I was in luck because Mrs. Murphy answered the door. She was so surprised and happy you would think it was the best present in the world. I heard one of the boys coughing and then he called, "Mom," in a weak voice. Mrs. Murphy sighed and said she had to go. I asked if they were awfully sick and she said, "Yes." I can't imagine them awfully sick. I thought they were the type that never in their lives got sick. At least they are well enough to look out the window today.

      This is a very medium day, a sort of low medium.

Thought for the day: Even very strong boys can get very sick.

Yours truly,

Gertrude

A very mysterious thing happened. When I got to the fence where the garden is I found a wooden box that somebody put right under the knot hole. That is kind of mysterious I think. I almost walked right past because I thought somebody put it there and so maybe somebody knows I stop and peek there and have to stand on my tip toes. But then I thought anybody could put that box there for no reason at all. So I stepped up on the box and then I didn't have to stand on tip toe but I had to bend down to look through the knot hole.

I saw something new. It was a small bush with yellow flowers on it. I couldn't see all of it because it is in a corner near the fence beside the shed. I had to twist my head way around to look. I like looking through the knot hole. It's like those pretty Easter eggs that have a window in them. I've never had one but I've seen them in stores and peeked inside and seen all sorts of little things. The more you look the more you see.

I finally got down from the box and went home. I bet if I stood up straight on that box I could see over the fence. But then if anybody was looking out of a window in the house they would see me. Then what would I do? I'd better not try.

I wore my new dress to school today and Sandra said, "Cute dress," when we were in line for recess. She is nice even if she is popular.

No Murphy boys outside playing. It is very peaceful but I wonder about them. It is even sort of mysterious. Where are the Murphy boys? Who put the box in the alley under the knot hole?

Thought for the day: Mysterious things are things you don't know the answer to.

Yours truly,

Gertrude

Today I found out something interesting about the number 9. It is a trick. The answer to 9 times anything always adds up to 9. Like 9x2 = 18. Then 1+8 = 9. It works every time except with 9 times 11. I can't figure that one out. But I think that's a very interesting thing for a number to be able to do.

I do not know whether to call these days good or medium. They are a little nicer than medium but nothing specially nice happens either. I am glad I have stopped looking for a friend. Someday I will find one and it will be like finding a penny or dime on the sidewalk. You don't look for pennies or dimes but then one day there one is. Only that doesn't happen very often.

Sandra said, "Hi," to me today for no reason. Mary Beth came up to me at recess, but when she saw I didn't have any candy she went away. I think I will wash Melinda Lou's clothes today.

Still no Murphy boys. It seems very empty in the backyard.

I didn't stop long at the garden because it was too windy and rainy and cold to do anything but shiver. I don't know how the flowers can stand it.

Thought for the day: Just because things look tender like flowers doesn't mean they can't stand things like cold weather.

Yours truly,

Gertrude

Today I found out many things. I found out that 9 works even when it's times 11. Because, 9x11 = 99. And 9+9 = 18. Then, 1+8 = 9. So it is perfect and works every time.

I found out that the Murphy boys are not dead of some awful sickness. They were all alive and sitting on the porch when I got home. They looked very limp. But they weren't completely limp. One of them was saying, "Ma, can't I take off this old hat? I'm hot," and Mrs. Murphy shouted, "You keep that hat on." While that was going on I got up the stairs but I think he kept his hat on. If they went to the same school I do I wonder which one of them would be in my room? I wonder what that would be like. I am glad they do not go to the same school.

Now I will tell the best thing. When I got to the garden and peeked through the knot hole I suddenly wished I could see more. I looked all around as much as I could through the knot hole. I looked at the house. Everything was quiet and I thought I'd take a chance. So I stood up tall and looked at the whole garden. It was very nice being so high up. I was looking and looking when suddenly the woman came out of the shed. I couldn't move. I was scared. But she just said, "Hello." I still didn't say anything. She said, "Come in and see my garden." So I did. Because she smiled.

She showed me some violets. They were around the corner of the shed under the bush with yellow flowers that I couldn't see very well from the knot hole.

I asked her about the white flowers and she said they were snowdrops. That is a perfect name for them because they grow in the snow.

I was going to ask her about the box under the knot hole but didn't.

She said her name was Mrs. Blonski and I said mine was Gertrude Kloppenberg. She said, "Do they call you Trudy?" I said, "No," but she said, "May I call you Trudy?" I said, "Yes."

Then she picked three violets and two violet leaves and gave them to me and said, "Come again anytime." And she smiled. I think she is a friend.

I took the violets home and found a little bottle that used to be a pill bottle and set the table and put the violets in the middle of the table. They are beautiful. The leaves are shaped like a heart. The purple is so pretty and soft.

Thought for the day: A person doesn't have to be your age to be a friend.

Yours truly,

Gertrude (Trudy to my friend)

Friday, April 12

There is no school today but Mother has to work. Today is Good Friday. I never understood why they called it Good Friday. I would call it Bad Friday.

Last night Mother brought me a dress. This is the second time she's done that. It is such a good surprise and it is such a pretty dress. It is plain and pink but looks very smart. That is what Mother says Miss Rice says. It is really Miss Rice's idea to buy dresses for me. Mother says it's a good buy and she is very happy. Also she says if she keeps listening to Miss Rice our budget will be ruined. I hope our budget isn't ruined.

I just tried on my new dress again and this time I dared to look in the mirror for a long time and really look at me. Now I know two things about me. I know I am not fat even if I do feel fat sometimes. Also I know I am not ugly. I am not pretty like a princess but I am not ugly like an ugly stepsister.

I went to the library today instead of tomorrow

43

like I usually do. Also I stopped at the best dime store and bought a chocolate egg with Mother written on it and some Easter egg dye and a little bottle with tiny egg-shaped candies all different colors. They will be Easter eggs for Melinda Lou. Saturday night I will hide them around her house in the bottom drawer of my dresser so she can have an Easter egg hunt too.

I think about Mrs. Blonski and her garden because it is cold and raining today. I would go just to see if the flowers were standing it but I have extra jobs to do so we will be ready for Easter. I had better do them now.

Thought for the day: It is interesting to get ready for special days like Easter.

Yours truly,

Gertrude (Trudy)

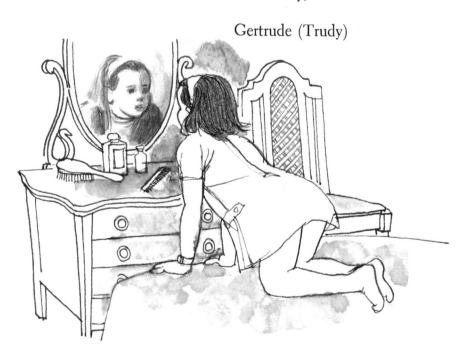

Monday, April 15

Easter was yesterday and there is no school today but Mother has to work. I will write in my book about yesterday and then I will go to Mrs. Blonski's garden. Today is nice and sunny and warm.

Yesterday was sunny but not warm. Miss Rice came to our house for dinner. Our Easter eggs looked nice. I wore my new dress and Miss Rice had a flowery hat. It was a special day.

Mother and Miss Rice did the dishes and I didn't have anything to do so I looked out the back window and watched the Murphy boys. They are interesting to watch if you don't have to be too close. First they were just running around. Then they threw Easter eggs to one another but they always caught them. Then they threw two at a time back and forth, throwing and catching and throwing again very fast. Still they didn't break any. They kept looking up but I was behind the curtain so they couldn't see me.

Next they got on one another's shoulders and threw eggs that way. Then they started getting silly and bumping one another and throwing eggs at one another and falling down and

running around until their father came out and yelled at them. He made them pick up all the broken eggs and sent them in the house and gave each one a hit as he went past. Nobody seemed to mind getting hit. I don't like getting hurt, but they don't care. I don't understand boys.

Then Mother and Miss Rice and I went to a conservatory. We had to go on two buses to get there. I have never seen such a beautiful place. It was very crowded but there were little places back from the walks that looked very private. One place had a water fall. It smelled damp and sweet. There were tons of tulips and daffodils.

Now I am going to Mrs. Blonski's. I guess I can't put what kind of day it is at the top because I haven't had it yet.

Thought for the day: Special days are very special.

Yours truly,

Gertrude (Trudy for short)

Tuesday, April 16

School today and it's cold and rainy. I wished it was yesterday because yesterday I spent the whole afternoon in Mrs. Blonski's garden. I told her about the conservatory and all the daffodils and tulips. She showed me her daffodils and tulips but they aren't blooming yet. The daffodils will bloom soon she said if the warm weather keeps up. Only it hasn't kept up.

Yesterday Mrs. Blonski let me dig and get the dirt ready for planting seeds. She showed me how. I saw some worms which were very crawly, but she said worms were good for gardens. It smelled so good, the dirt and the growing things and the sun. I guess sun smells.

Today Sandra said, "Hi," again. I think I will call her a friend even though she's not an only friend. At least she is not not a friend.

I stopped at the garden and the wooden box was still there so I stood up on it and looked over the fence. The daffodils aren't blooming. The house looked dark, but then I saw Mrs. Blonski in a window. She waved and I waved and then I went home.

The Murphy boys were on their back porch scraping mud off their shoes when I got home. I tried to ignore them and acted deaf but I heard them. They had a new thing to say. It was Gertrude the prude. How can they find so many awful things to say? Then I heard the biggest one, Bob, say, "Shut up," to his brothers. I felt glad and sort of safe. Even if he isn't a friend maybe he isn't an all out enemy.

Thought for the day: Not being an enemy is part way being a friend.

Yours truly,

Gertrude (Trudy)

Today I looked at the daffodils again but they didn't bloom. I didn't think they would because it is still cold and rainy. But the buds looked more yellow than green I think. I stood on the box. I was going to go home but Mrs. Blonski came to the back door and waved and asked me to come in. Her house is very small and smells like she cooks a lot of cabbage.

She showed me the plants she is growing in her house. All kinds in boxes. She said they were seedlings and she would put some where I dug for her. I thought she had said seeds but she had said seedlings. She talks sort of thick and I don't think I always know what she says.

She said when the daffodils bloomed she would give me some to take to school to my teacher. I don't know what Miss Hurly would do if I brought her some flowers. Would I have the nerve to do it? But I said, "Thank you," to

Mrs. Blonski because it was nice of her. I thought I'd think about would I dare take flowers to the teacher later.

She told me the names of all the little seedlings. But there were so many that I don't remember them except marigold, which I think is a very pretty name.

No Murphy boys so I don't know if their big brother cured them of calling names or not.

This could be a good day I think, except the weather was bad which makes it only a medium day.

Thought for the day: Weather can sometimes make days good or bad or medium.

Yours truly,

Gertrude (Trudy)

Thursday, April 18

I was right yesterday about the weather making days good or bad because today was warm and sunny and everyone seemed happy and everything went well.

Sandra asked me to play jump rope at recess. I just turned because I don't jump very well. I was afraid I'd get all tangled up and fall and hurt myself. But I turn very well. I watched how the best jumpers jumped and I am going to practice in private.

The daffodils are blooming and Mrs. Blonski says tomorrow morning I should stop on my way to school and she will have some ready for me. I couldn't tell her I wasn't sure I wanted to take them. So I said I would stop on my way to school tomorrow. We sat on her bench and watched the daffodils nodding their heads in the breeze. It was very nice and pretty and private but I started thinking about jumping rope so I said good-bye and went home.

The littlest Murphy was in the yard, hanging by his knees from the fence. "Look at me. Look at me," he kept saying so I couldn't ignore him. I said, "I see you." Then he fell down on his head but he just laughed and rolled over and kicked his legs and laughed some more. I laughed too. If he hurt himself he didn't act like it. Boys must be very tough. Little Jimmy by himself is kind of cute.

Now I have to find my jump rope and practice.

Thought for the day: One person can be better than a bunch, especially if they're boys.

Yours truly,

Gertrude (Trudy)

I started to school early this morning. The sun was warm but the breeze around my legs was still cool. Mrs. Blonski had a bunch of daffodils ready for me. The stems were wrapped in waxpaper and tied with a string. I was glad I was early. I went in before the bell and gave them to Miss Hurly who was very surprised. Then I went out to the playground again. Nobody would have known it was me who brought the flowers except when we were all seated Miss Hurly said, "See the lovely flowers Gertrude Kloppenberg brought." My face got all hot and everyone turned around and looked at me.

At recess I turned for jump rope again. I still don't know how to jump. I found my old jump rope but when I tried to jump in the house everything rattled. I don't know where to practice. I can't practice outside even in our alley because of the Murphys. Maybe I could practice on the way home except I usually carry books. Maybe if I hurry very fast I can do all my work in school and not carry books and then I can practice on the way. I'll try that Monday.

Also Sandra said the daffodils were very pretty and she wished she had some flowers. I wondered if it was like Mary Beth and the candy but then I remembered Sandra was friendly before I had any flowers. I'm glad she likes flowers. Someday I'll ask Mrs. Blonski if Sandra can see her garden. But what if Sandra doesn't want to? I'll think about that.

I stopped at the garden and told Mrs. Blonski how happy the teacher was with the daffodils. She showed me how fast her seedlings are growing and how fast everything outside is growing with all the sun and warm weather. With Mrs. Blonski telling me to look I see things I might never see, like fat lilac buds.

No Murphys. Not even Jimmy.

Thought for the day: More people than you think like flowers.

Yours truly,

Gertrude (Trudy)

Monday, April 22

Today at recess I just turned the rope again. I was tired of just turning the rope. I was tired of not finding a place to practice. I thought about learning to jump rope all Saturday and Sunday. I even carried my jump rope to school and didn't have any books but I was afraid to try on the way to school. I thought I would probably always have to just turn all the rest of my life. But after school I stopped at Mrs. Blonski's.

It was an almost hot day. She stopped working in her garden and we sat on her bench. She asked me about school. I told her about not jumping rope which I meant to keep secret. But I told her.

Mrs. Blonski said she used to be a good jump roper. She took my rope and jumped. We laughed and laughed. She is sort of big around the middle and too old to jump, but she jumped. Then I took a turn. We laughed some more when I got tangled up. She took another turn and showed me how to take a little jump between the big jumps. I did better and better. Then she showed me how to jump first one foot and then the other like skipping. Then she showed me the best. It's like running and jumping rope at the same time. It is hard but I could do it most of the time. Mrs. Blonski said with practice I would be good and that I was a natural born jump roper. I went up and down her walk and it was almost like flying.

I finally went home. I even tried jumping on the way and I could do it. Now I have to hurry and get my jobs done. This day turned out better than it started so I think I will call it a good day.

Thought for the day: Some days that start out bad end up good.

Yours truly,

Gertrude (Trudy)

Today at school I still just turned because I got to thinking that jumping a big rope was different than jumping by yourself and maybe I couldn't do it.

I asked Mrs. Blonski after school and she said it was different. She got a clothesline and tied it to a post. Then she turned one end and I practiced.

Then Mrs. Blonski's son came home. He is a man. He had on a white jacket and white pants because he is going to be a doctor. He took the other end. I felt funny but he smiled like Mrs. Blonski smiles and I jumped.

Then we took turns and he even took a turn only he didn't jump very well. He just stood there and when the rope came down he gave a hop. Mrs. Blonski tried to teach him. She said it was like dancing and you didn't go clomp, clomp, clomp. But he said he wasn't a dancer or a jumper and he'd be a turner. We laughed a lot and it was fun.

Mrs. Blonski's son is the nicest man I've ever seen. His name is Carl. He called me Trudy because Mrs. Blonski said that's what my name was.

Now I have to hurry and do my jobs.

Thought for the day: Carl Blonski is a nice man.

Yours truly,

Trudy

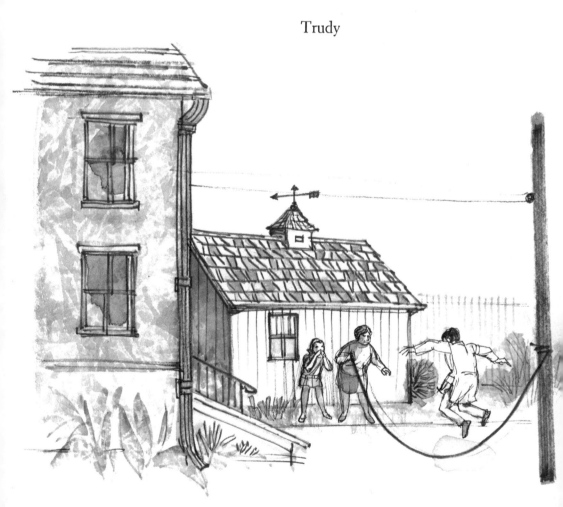

Today I jumped rope at school but it wasn't easy. At first when I said I wanted to jump nobody listened. They thought I was just going to be a turner the rest of my life, I could tell. But I said it again and Sandra said, "I'll turn. Get in line." After that everybody took turns jumping and turning when the one before missed. I didn't miss once. They were surprised.

After school I told Mrs. Blonski how good I jumped. She was glad. She showed me some pansies she had planted near the tulips. The tulip buds are changing from little green pointed things to bigger redder ones. Mrs. Blonski says some years you wait and wait for things to bloom and then it gets hot and everything comes at once like a blaze. She said she would give me some tulips for school and they would be ready if it was another warm day tomorrow.

What I like best is the pansies. They are so soft and

have such pretty faces like little pouty animals. Each color makes a different face. Each one is so beautiful I could never choose which was best. I could watch them forever. Mrs. Blonski gave me three and told me to put water in a dish and float the pansies in the water, which I have now done and set the table with them in the middle.

I haven't seen any Murphys except Jimmy who always says, "Hi," now. Today he said, "What you got?" and I showed him. The others probably stay at school and play baseball. At least that's what the boys at our school do.

Thought for the day: You can look at beautiful things forever.

Yours truly,

Trudy

It was very warm again today but it wasn't sunny. It was a strange day. It felt like something was going to happen.

After school Mrs. Blonski said it was a thunderstorm that was going to happen. We sat on her bench. It was very still in the garden but we watched up high in the sky and clouds went by very fast.

The tulips are ready and Mrs. Blonski said to stop on my way to school tomorrow. Then she said to hurry home before the storm started.

By the time I got near home big drops started. The wind blew and children were running and doors slamming and mothers calling and I ran. It was very exciting. I got home safely and it was very dark. Now it is raining hard with thunder and lightning. It makes it feel cozy inside.

I think I will read that book that I have been too busy jumping rope to read. I was going to read it right away

because it is a special book. The girl I keep seeing at the library said to me when I was looking on the shelf for books, "This is a good book." I took it and said, "Thanks." I should have told her about a good book but I couldn't think in time. I think of her as my library friend without a name. I hope the book is good because she said it was.

Thought for the day: It is nice to have a house in a storm.

Yours truly,

Trudy

I took the tulips to school this morning and Miss Hurly was very happy again. All morning she called on me extra times and gave me a special smile every time which made me feel very uncomfortable. Maybe when Mrs. Blonski was a girl people took flowers to school but I'm the only one I know that ever takes flowers to the teacher. I wonder if maybe I shouldn't. At recess I heard a girl say, "She thinks she's so smart, taking flowers to the teacher." Meaning me.

    I think it was better when nobody noticed me. I didn't have friends but I didn't have enemies. Sandra was nice about the flowers because she was interested. She said she wished she had flowers. I saw her stop at the teacher's desk after recess and look at the tulips specially. I decided to ask Mrs. Blonski if I can bring Sandra to see the garden. So I asked Mrs. Blonski after school and she said to bring Sandra any time. So Monday I'll ask Sandra and see.

Mrs. Blonski's garden is prettier and prettier. I went around and looked at each flower. She has a tree that is getting flowers on it, apple blossoms. She said everything is early this year. She showed me her seedlings again. They are bigger. She said she would set them out soon. I asked if I could help and she said that I could. The marigolds had little buds. I don't know about marigold's smell. They don't have a good smell. It isn't sweet like other flowers. It tickles your nose and is sort of sharp. I like it and I don't like it.

Now I am going to finish reading that book. It is good.

Thought for the day: Spring is beautiful.

Yours truly,

Trudy

Today I asked Sandra if she would like to see Mrs. Blonski's garden. She said she would ask her mother and maybe we could see it tomorrow. She was very glad and she talked about it twice more during the day. I was surprised that she got so excited about seeing a garden. I thought popular people didn't get excited about things like gardens.

Yesterday Miss Rice borrowed her brother's car and took Mother and me to see a tulip festival. It was far away in a suburb. I don't think I had ever been so far away before. There were bunches of tulips, all colors. I didn't know tulips came in so many colors. We walked around and walked around. There were lots of people. It was pretty but it was almost too much. I think I like little gardens that are private best.

After school I told Mrs. Blonski about all the tulips at the festival and she said in Holland they have fields and fields of tulips and one time when the people were starving they had to eat the tulip bulbs. She told me what a tulip bulb was like because I didn't know about bulbs. I wonder if I could eat a tulip bulb and know it would mean I was really eating a beautiful flower.

Also I told Mrs. Blonski about Sandra and she said. "Good." I helped her dig along the walk that goes from her gate to her back door. That is where she puts the marigolds, all along it. I like getting the dirt all smooth and crumbling up the lumps and patting and spreading it around. I never thought I would think dirt was so nice.

Thought for the day: Dirt is nice.

Yours truly,

Trudy

Today Sandra went to Mrs. Blonski's with me after school. She was still very excited. On the way I showed her how I could run and jump rope because I never before had a chance to show anyone. It's too crowded at school. I let her try with my rope because she didn't have a rope. She said she would bring her rope to school tomorrow and we could show the other girls.

When we got to Mrs. Blonski's garden Sandra kept saying, "How pretty." Mrs. Blonski smiled and smiled. I wondered if I had told Mrs. Blonski enough how pretty I thought it was. But Mrs. Blonski winked at me like we knew something that Sandra didn't. Then I didn't mind sharing our private garden with her.

Mrs. Blonski said that tomorrow was May Day and when she was little they made May baskets and put flowers in them and hung them on friends' doorknobs the night before and surprised them. Sandra said that the olden days must have

been very nice. Mrs. Blonski laughed and told us that, yes, the olden days were good and they were bad, too, where she came from. She looked sad when she said bad. Then she said she would give us some flowers and we could make May baskets if we wanted. That made Sandra and me excited and we talked about how to make May baskets out of paper.

Then Mrs. Blonski said, "But flowers you pick don't last. If I give you a plant would you take care of it? Would you have a place to plant it?" We thought. I don't know what Sandra thought but I thought very hard and couldn't think of a place safe enough for a plant. Then I thought of a corner next to the fence so I said, "Yes."

Sandra said, "I bet everyone in the whole room would like to have a plant." Sandra always thinks about other people. And then she must have thought of Mrs. Blonski because she said, "I don't mean you should give them," and she stopped talking. But Mrs. Blonski said, "'That would be good. How many in your room?" I was surprised and Sandra was too. Sandra knew how many and said, "Twenty-seven."

71

Mrs. Blonski said, "Let's see about pots." We went into the shed and there were lots of little pots stacked up in a corner. Mrs. Blonski counted them and said, "Twenty-five." "Maybe everybody doesn't want a plant," I said.

Then Carl Blonski looked in the shed and said, "What are you girls up to?" and he said especially to me, "How's my jump roper?"

Mrs. Blonski told Carl about giving plants to everybody in our room but Carl said, "Don't give them, sell them. People appreciate what they pay for more than what's just given to them." Mrs. Blonski said that she had more plants than she needed and why not give them to the children. We had to talk and talk about it. Carl called it palaver. That is a good word. It means talk and talk and talk, Carl says.

Finally we decided. We are going to charge 3¢ a plant and tomorrow we are going to ask Miss Hurly and let kids sign up. After school I will help Mrs. Blonski put them in pots. Sandra can't because on Monday, Wednesday, and Friday she has to take care of her little brother and fix dinner because her mother works. I didn't know she had to do things like that.

Then Carl had to go back to the hospital where I guess he lives most of the time. I walked most of the way back to school with Sandra. I knew if I lived way on the other side of the school she'd walk part way with me. Then I had to run most of the way back home and do my jobs. The Murphys were there but I hardly knew it until I was passed. I was going so fast.

Thought for the day: Spring is a very busy time.

Yours truly,

Trudy

Today is May Day and we forgot about May baskets. We were so busy talking about plants. At recess we talked to Miss Hurly about the plants and she thought it was a good idea. We didn't even jump rope we were so busy.

Sandra wrote on top of a piece of paper:

I WOULD LIKE TO BUY A MARIGOLD
PLANT FOR 3¢—SIGN BELOW

After recess Sandra told the class about the plants. Then I passed the piece of paper around the room. Twenty-five kids signed. We couldn't figure out who didn't sign. We went over and over the list and finally thought—it was us who didn't sign. Sandra and I decided we could have a plant without a pot.

After school I went to Mrs. Blonski's and helped put the plants in pots. Twenty-five is a lot. We worked and worked and it suddenly got very cold. I worried about the plants but Mrs. Blonski said plants could stand the change in weather more than people and I should go home and she would finish. But I stayed even though I got very shivery. We finally got them all in pots and watered them.

I put a sweater on when I got home but I am still cold and now I sneezed. I had better not catch a cold. There is too much to do. Tomorrow Mrs. Blonski is going to tell us what to tell the kids about how to take care of their plants.

Now I will do my jobs and maybe that will stop me shivering.

Thought for the day: Sometimes weather can change too fast.

Yours truly,

Trudy

I did catch cold but I acted like I was well even though I didn't feel like it. Mother said maybe I should stay home but then said all right I could go. She hates to leave me alone. I've only got a cold, anyway.

Taking care of plants is very complicated. Sandra and I went to Mrs. Blonski's and she told us a whole lot of things. Sandra wrote them all down. Then we filled little envelopes with white powder that's supposed to help when you plant the plant in the ground. The powder is for the roots so they'll grow specially. Then we filled more little envelopes with green stuff like sugar and that's food for the plants to help them be healthy. "Like vitamin pills," Carl said.

Then Carl said, "How are you going to get all those pots to school?" We palavered about that and Carl said one of his friends at the hospital had a car and Carl and his friend with the car would bring them in the afternoon.

After a long time we had everything ready and I went home. I walked part way back toward school with Sandra. She was still very excited about the marigold plants. All of the plants have buds and some of them have little flowers. We decided to hand them out in order (that is going to be my job) and whoever comes next will get the next one whether it has flowers or not.

After I said good-bye to Sandra I was sorry I was so far away from home. I wished I was home because I felt shivery. But now I am home and must do my jobs in a hurry if I can.

Thought for the day: Taking care of plants is very complicated.

Yours truly,

Trudy

Everything is over and it has been a very exciting day. Carl and his friend brought the plants to school and everyone said, "Who's that?" And I said, "He's my friend."

Sandra read the rules. She acted just like a teacher and had everyone get out pencil and paper and copy down the rules for planting marigolds. When she came to the part about the powder for the roots I passed out the envelopes full of powder. Then at the right time I passed out the envelopes of plant food. Then Sandra checked off the names on the list and I took the money and handed out the plants. Then we were through.

After school we went to Mrs. Blonski's. Sandra said she could go if she hurried even though it was her day to take care of her little brother. So she got her plant without the pot. Mrs. Blonski had it all wrapped up in wet newspaper and then wax paper. We gave Mrs. Bronski the money—75¢ mostly in

pennies. But Mrs. Blonski said, no, that we should share. But they were her flowers we said. But finally we each took 25¢. Sandra had to go. Then I took my plant without the pot and went home to plant it. I remembered to bring my ruler from school because one of the rules was to dig the dirt eight inches deep before you plant the marigold.

When I got home the backyard was full of boys. The Murphys had a chair and table in the yard and a pitcher full of pink drink and lots of glasses. "Come on," they said. "Buy a cherry drink for 3¢." Everyone was jumping around

but it was different. They weren't jumping at me, just around. I had my pennies from the plants in my pocket so I bought a drink. I had hardly had any to drink when Mrs. Murphy came home and said, "What's going on here?" Then she went in the house with her groceries. But she came right out again and said, "You get in here and clean up this mess right now." She looked awfully mad. Everyone left and the Murphy boys hardly sassed back at all. I put down my glass and went upstairs.

When the yard was all quiet and empty I went back down and dug the dirt until it was all soft for eight inches down. Then I planted my marigold and poured water with the white powder in it around the roots. It looked awfully small and limp in its corner by the fence but Mrs. Blonski said it will grow and spread.

Now I am finished with everything but my jobs. I think I want to sit down and put my feet up like Mother does when she gets home from work extra tired. Also my chest hurts when I cough. But I try not to cough.

Thought for the day: When excitement is over you feel very tired.

Yours truly,

Trudy

Saturday, May 4

I never write in my book on Saturday but today is a different Saturday so I am writing in it. Mother had to go to work today. She didn't want to go to work but she had to. It is a special time because they are closing the books, she said. Also she said we were lucky she didn't always have to work on Saturday because she was in bookkeeping and not a saleswoman. She has said that before.

I was asleep when Mother got home yesterday. She helped me get to bed and made me some soup which I only ate a little of. I told her I was too tired and she said I had been overdoing. This morning she woke me up to say she was going and I should stay in bed. I did. I slept till ten o'clock and then I got up to see how my plant was. It is fine. It is not so limp anymore.

It was hot down in the yard and my eyes hurt in the sun so I came back upstairs and didn't know what to do. I thought of my private book and when I got it I saw poor Melinda Lou who I have mostly forgot all about. Poor Melinda Lou. She is a very old doll that someday I will give to my little girl, Mother says. I suppose she is used to just waiting to be played with but I thought I would always and forever play with her.

Now I am writing in my book but I think I will stop because I can't keep it up. I don't feel like me. And the Murphys are downstairs shouting around about some game about who's king of the fence. And shouting at Jimmy to hold the corner. What corner? My plant. I'd better see about my plant.

I put stars all over the top of the page because it is the first time in a long time that I can write in my private book. I read what I last wrote in the book. I didn't finish writing that day, and now I am going to tell what happened next, but I hate to think about it.

Well, after I heard the Murphys shouting I jumped up and ran downstairs. I was right. They were jumping on my plant. It was Jimmy. I was so mad. I didn't know myself I was so mad. I screamed at him and ran over and started hitting him. I hit him and hit him. It was awful. And the bigger Murphys stood around and cheered. They like a fight. But I couldn't stop hitting him once I started. Then his brothers shouted, "Hey, he's littler than you." I stopped and screamed, "I don't care. He ruined my plant." One of them said, "You're crazy to plant a plant in our backyard." I felt crazy.

I wanted to run upstairs and throw myself on my

bed and cry and cry but they were all lined up between me and
the stairs. There was no escape but through the gate and down
the alley. I ran. I ran to Mrs. Blonski's. But I don't know how
I got there. But I remember telling her, "My plant is ruined.
My plant is ruined," over and over. She hugged me and said,
"There, there." Then she said, "I think you're sick," and took

me in the house and made me lie down. Then I remember Carl bending over me and whispering to his mother. After that what I remember is all jumbled up like a bad dream. But now I know what happened.

They took me to the hospital and I was very sick with pneumonia. I had to have an oxygen tent which I think I

remember a little. I remember seeing my mother once sitting by my bed looking very sad. I tried to tell her not to worry but I don't know what I really said.

I don't remember anything else much that happened until I started getting well. Now I am all well except for being weak. And I am home. I have been home two days. I thought about writing in my book but it seemed too hard. But now I am doing it. But I am tired from writing so much so I will tell the rest tomorrow.

Yours truly,

Trudy

Today I am dressed. I feel like a stranger in my clothes. It has been so long since I wore them. I don't think I feel so weak today, just strange. Mother says not to overdo but I don't think writing in my book is overdoing so I will write all the rest of what happened.

What I remember most about the hospital, after I started getting well, is the nice nurses. I think I will be a nurse. They smile and rub your back and take your temperature and smile some more and ask you if you're comfortable and they have such nice cool hands. I wonder if my hands would be cool enough.

Carl Blonski came in to see me many times at the hospital and his nurse friend did too. Her name is Irene. They were both very nice to me but more interested in seeing each other than seeing me, I could tell. They would look at one another more than at me. Then one of them would say some-

thing to me, and then the other would remember and say something to me. Irene is very pretty and I don't blame Carl for
liking her. I bet they get married and when they have children
Carl will jump rope with them.

Mrs. Blonski came one day and brought a big big

pot full of marigold plants. Carl said that was a very special thing his mother did because she doesn't go many places. I almost cried I was so happy to see her.

Also the teacher sent me letters from everyone in the class. They mostly said, "Sorry you're sick," and "Get well soon." But Sandra's letter was long and she told me about her marigold plant which is doing very well and she takes very good care of it.

Now it is later because Mrs. Blonski and Carl came to see me. They brought a window box with some dirt in it. They helped me plant the marigold plants that Mrs. Blonski gave me in the hospital. The plants look very nice and they will be safe in the window box on our window sill. Mrs. Blonski told me to come and see her garden as soon as I was up to it because she has peonies and iris blooming. I don't know what those plants are but she said they were very pretty. Carl said I could go to school Monday but not to start jumping rope yet. He said, "Even if you are a champion jumper," and we all laughed. Then they had to go.

Now I think maybe I did overdo. I am very tired of getting tired so I will rest and maybe next time I get up I won't get so tired. I was going to write much more but I can't think what.

Thought for the day: People are very nice to you when you are sick but it is awful to be sick.

Yours truly,

Trudy

Later the same day

After I slept for a long while I woke up and heard a knock, knock, very quiet, at the back door. I put on my robe and went to see. It was Jimmy. He said, "Hi. I'm sorry you're

90

sick." He looked quiet and shy. I remembered that awful day. I said, "Did I hurt you very much?" He smiled and said, "Aw, naw, girls can't hurt me." I told him I was glad. He told me that Tom said I was a good fighter when I was mad. Then he said that I could have a plant in the backyard if I wanted and

nobody would jump on it. That made me feel very good. I thought that maybe I could plant one of my marigolds in the backyard. Maybe I could put a little fence around it, I thought. Then I remembered how it is in the backyard most of the time and how the Murphys are always jumping around. So I just said, "Thank you but I think I'll grow my plants in my window box. But thank you." I think Jimmy thought that was best too because he just said, "Okay," and went away. Now I know the Murphy boys aren't mean. They're just the rough type. We'll never be friends but we won't be enemies. That is, out and out enemies. They'll probably tease me because that is their way. But I won't be scared, I think.

Second thought for the day: There are many types of people in the world and even if you can't like them you don't have to be enemies, I think.

Yours truly,

Trudy

Today was a special day in many ways. First be-cause I went outside and walked to Mrs. Blonski's. I felt very well inside but my legs aren't that well yet. They felt limp. I saw Mrs. Blonski's peonies and iris and they are beautiful. The peonies smell sweet. Then Mrs. Blonski walked back home with me to see that I got home safe.

I was happy but tired when I got home. It is good to go outside again. I took a nap, like Mrs. Blonski told me. When I woke up it was after school time and I heard the Murphys downstairs shouting around. Then I listened to what they were shouting. They were teasing someone, saying, "Missy Prissy," and "Miss Stuck Up." I went to see who it was. It was Sandra.

I went out on the back porch and I made my hands into fists even though I knew I could never fight them. I put one fist on my hip and held the other one up where they could

see it and shouted, "You leave her alone. She's my friend."
Then the Murphys acted like they were scared of me and bowed
and opened the gate for Sandra and said, "Please don't hurt
us," and hid behind their hands.

Sandra who I thought always knew what to do
looked like she didn't know what to do so I called down,
"Come on up, don't mind them. Their bark is worse than
their bite." I never should have said that because then they

started barking and howling and acting like dogs. Sandra came on upstairs. She ran the last way just like I always felt like doing. I held the door open for her and we ran in and slammed it. It was very exciting. We almost collapsed laughing.

The Murphys are really funny. But we decided the best thing to do is ignore them. So that's how we are going to do it and only laugh in private about the funny things they do.

I was surprised to see Sandra especially on Friday

95

but she said a neighbor was taking care of her little brother so she could come and see me. She also said she missed me. I was surprised again and said, "But you have so many friends." She told me that she had a lot of friends all right but no special friend and would I be her special friend. I could hardly believe her but I said right off, "Yes, I would like that."

We talked a long time about being special friends. When she had to go I stood on the back porch and waved to her and the Murphys waved to her and said in high silly voices, "Good-bye Sandra." But she just held her head up high and paid no attention.

I am going to put a great big star on the top today and put marks around it because it has been such a special day because I now have a special friend. She will be a true blue friend, I know, like in that book I read.

Thought for the day: Some books that you think could never be true sometimes can be true.

Yours truly,

Trudy